The Legend of Dogdog!

Natalie Thurman

The Legend of Dogdog!

Written and Illustrated by Natalie Thurman

This is dedicated to all the brave pets of the 2020 lockdown and to Oliver Morgan, Winnie and Rose Nadin.

Thank you to all the dog owners who gave permission for me to include their pets.

Have you heard of Dogdog?

So the legend goes, he is the bravest of brave dogs who follows his nose.

His coat is shiny
and his nose his
wet.

This friendly pup,
enjoys a trip to the
vet.

Have you seen
Dogdog?

So the legend
goes, he is the
goodest of good
dogs who follows
his nose.

He walks to heel
and responds to
recall.

To get him to
play, you just
throw him his ball.

He never runs
away and never
pulls on the lead.

He trots by your
side and adjusts to
your speed.

Have you met Dogdog?

So the legend goes, he is the largest of large dogs who follows his nose.

This gregarious
dog, does not fit
into clothes.

He has style and
grace and this
really shows.

Have you spied
Dogdog?

So the legend goes,
he is the strangest
of strange dogs
who follows his
nose.

He likes to eat sticks, eat socks and eat shoes.

You see all the evidence, when you look at his poos.

Have you noticed
Dogdog?

So the legend goes,
he is the smartest
of smart dogs who
follows his nose.

He loves to read
the news, play
puzzles and games.

When it comes to
"I Spy" he knows
all the names.

He understands
lie, paw and sit.

He drops what he
has, if you ask him
"leave it."

Have you witnessed Dogdog?

So the legend goes, he is the friendliest of friendly dogs who follows his nose.

When he sees
another dog, he
runs over to say
"Hi!"

He never wants to
say "Goodbye."

Have you glimpsed
Dogdog?

So the legend goes,
he is the wisest of
wise dogs who
follows his nose.

He is brave, good, large, strange, smart, friendly and wise....

Perhaps he is your dog and just in disguise?

Or just maybe he is
your cat?

What do you think
of that...?

KC

Special thanks
to our pets
including

Poppy Bingo and Bubbles

Magneto

Sherlock

Ben

Finn

Stanley

Mystique

Lily

Dexter

Rufo

Ariel

Satchmo

Hugo

Abbie

Piper

Molly

Lola

Pippa

Printed in Great Britain
by Amazon